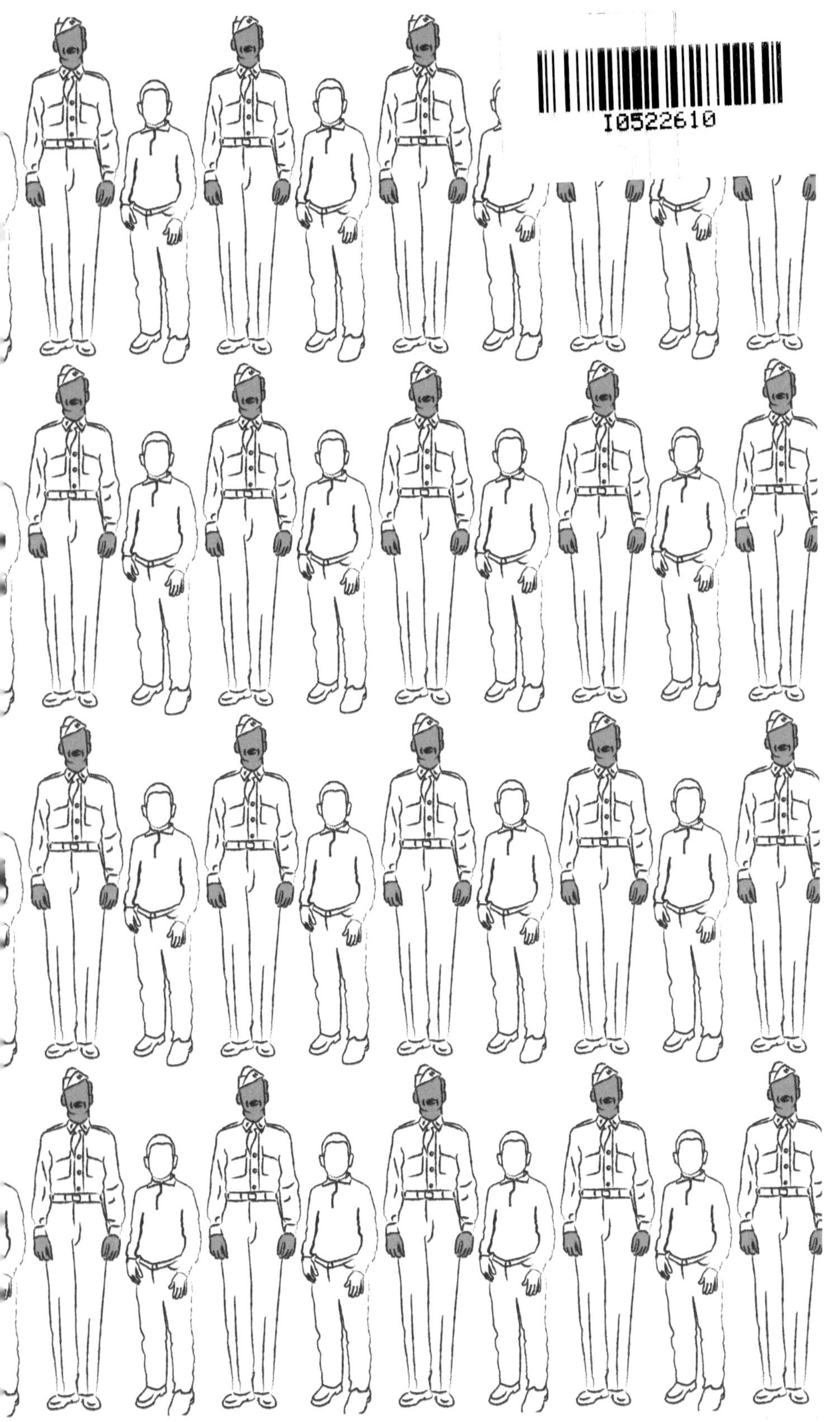

I0522610

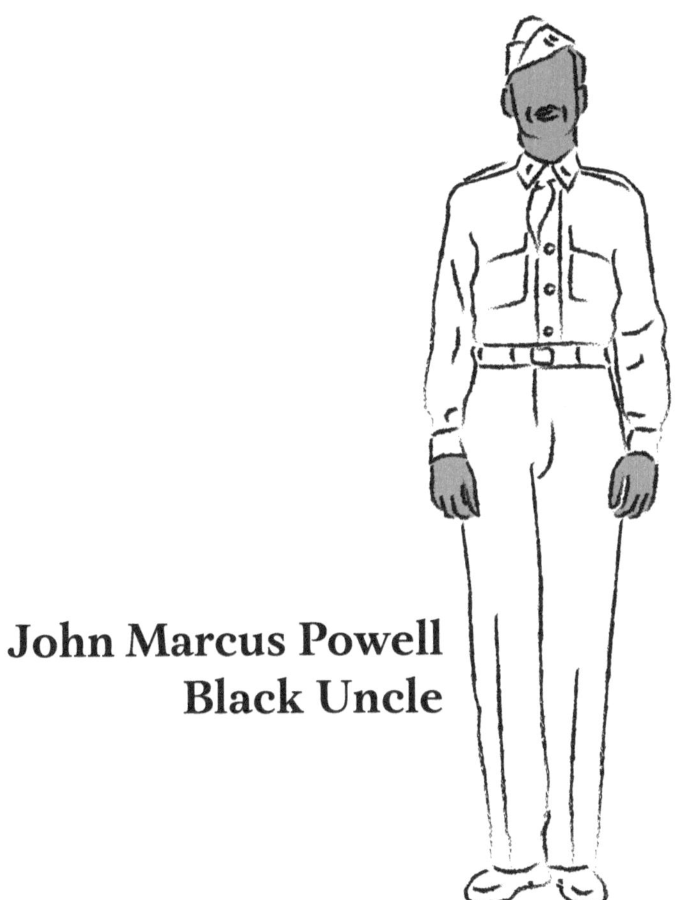

John Marcus Powell
Black Uncle

exotbooks.com
First Edition
Copyright 2022 John Marcus Powell
All Rights Reserved
Typeset in: Adonis & Aria Text G2
ISBN: 978-0-9898984-6-1

Editing — R. Nemo Hill
Design & Interior Illustrations — Julian M. Perea
Cover Art — Murray Simpson - GARENNE 2017
Back Cover Art — Murray Simpson - (detail) A CITY GARDEN IN MAY

John Marcus Powell and I share a generation and a geography.
I opened this book and turned the pages greedily, drawn into a
story told in an irresistible voice that leads, like the pied piper,
into a way of life that has almost disappeared. The poem begins
at a moment frozen in history but the protagonist steps from it
into our changed society with the abiding truth of boyhood held
out like a perfectly-wrapped gift.

— Ann Drysdale, author of *Feeling Unusual*

Reminiscent of Brian Friel's *Faith Healer*, John Marcus Powell's
Black Uncle is an intimate history told in voices—in this case a
Welsh boy named Timmy and his Mam. Their alternating mono-
logues tell a rich and nuanced tale of a family separated by the
Second World War and of the black American soldier who deeply
touches both of their lives. Powell orchestrates notes of personal
tragedy, parochial prejudice, and sexual awakening in delightful,
fluent verse, each line composed in the mouth of a brilliant ac-
tor-poet. When, years ago, I first heard Powell perform his poems
in a burlesque house in the East Village, I remember the buzz that
went around the room: here was the real deal! *Black Uncle* is his
strongest work to date, a tour de force of voice, character, and
feeling. I can't recommend it highly enough.

— David Yezzi, author of *More Things in Heaven: New and Se-
lected Poems*

John Marcus Powell brings a lost world marvelously back to life
again in *Black Uncle*, a world of fears, injuries, and losses caused
by poverty, war, and nonconformity. Yet, in the midst of great
deprivations in a tiny Welsh village, Powell celebrates the growth
of "exuberant weeds,/ extravagant brussel sprouts." Fans of Mar-
tina Evans's verse novels will love John Marcus Powell's *Black
Uncle*.

— Jee Leong Koh, author of *Inspector Inspector*

For

Constance Powell

Table of Contents

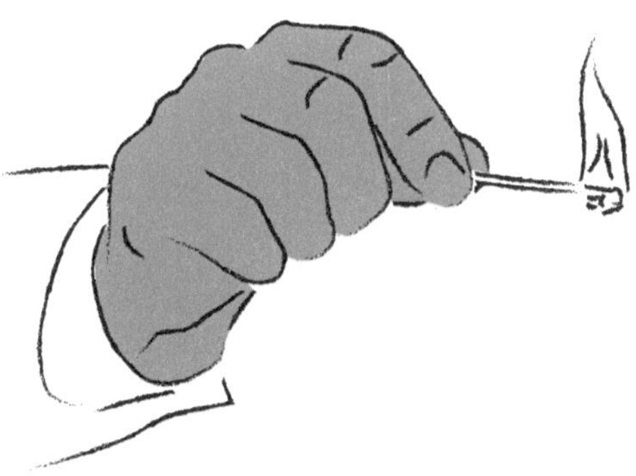

BOY

I am a little kid and I climb a tree.
There are all manner of trees in the village
which I get up on afternoons,
like the hollow tree in the hut ground, the pleasure ground,
called *hut ground* because of the hut at the center
where were held pleasurable festivities—
but that hollow tree is such an easy tree,
once up, you'd think you'd done nothing.

This one is different,
a tall elm covered in ivy,
its first branches a long way from the ground.
I claw my way up
muttering,
"It's too much for a boy my age
to have the necessary know-how,
but if it has to be done it has to be done."

The tree stands in the hedge of our back garden.
We have another garden at the front.
Front garden swoops down
towards church, river, fields.
Back garden slopes up a bank.

On one side a cow meadow,
on the other side the village street.
At the bottom side our little house.
Our house wants to wander,
but my Mam has given it instructions to stay put—
at the top side a stretching towards the school,
and beyond the school a yearning to the Main Road.

Along this Main Road march World Armies,
could be *our boys,* could be *Italian i'tis,* could be *Nazis.*
Across the main road, among the hills,

are incestuous villages.
Incestuous
is getting wild among trees with too many animals.
This definition endures.

Once up to the first branches,
to the left in Dai Evans' meadow
I see the limpid, patterned,
show-you-my-ass-to-see-poop-splattering
whole-face long-nostril breathing-blaring
eyes-looking-for-friendship cows—
static,
unlike the street the other side of me
running eternally till it turns left at the school.
At the school, I'm learning why *left* is *left*, *right right*,
how *is* is *is*, how *was* is *was*.

After the school, the street bends
to the Main Road.
Wider than the village street, it deserves to be Main—
for when I stand at the junction waiting for a bus,
potent is the tarmac with convoys due to come
as well as ones belonging to my small past.

If the convoys come from the left
they are coming from the direction of the town.
If they come from the right
they are coming from the direction of Gran's house,
three miles longer along.
Coming from Gran's, the drivers of trucks tanks jeeps
pass through the *King of Prussia* pub.
After getting drunk in the pub's dark rooms,
they veer out against God's wishes,
bounding off the skies,
rolling past the bus-stop

where quiet women wait loudly for the bus.

"They're English," says Mrs. Irish Pat,
whose husband's at the front
(and it's him that's Irish and not herself).
Blond, working in the town hospital,
she's wearing a good shopping outfit
cos she's still young
and she's going out to market on the bus.

My Mam says, "They're American.
The English ones,
they don't stand that high up."

Oppy Pritchard, headmistress,
with a dark limp and a brimmed hat,
says categorically, "They're trucks
bringing the Italian prisoners of war
back from the fields.
They know more than us
about agriculture—
what with their vines and their rice."

If getting up the tree has been difficult,
getting down is desperate.
I clutch at the trunk too broad to be clutchable,
and the ivy, frailer than when I ascended, breaks off.
I'm living in a huddle of scuffs and grazes,
convinced that what I'm doing
goes beyond all notion
of tree, of war, of climb.
                    To concentrate,
all but the immediate must be forgot.

Church and river fields hide behind the house.

Outside vision, they can't be grasped.
On any weekday, the church is best left for Sundays,
and the river fields with the railway line
streaking the river bridge for Cardiff
are best left for Hitler—
a man anxious to destroy *all means of communication,*
one who sends his pilots over in the night.

I don't fall.
I haven't fallen.
As I descend,
saplings in the hedge rise
with leaves, feathery.
Anticipation is heavy.
There's going to be a jolt out of the hedge,
a dance down the bank,
a run out the gate
to get a drink of water
from the tap dribbling
on the out-sized stone placed under
to adequately support water buckets
of villagers with no inside tap
who collect water on the village street.

But this jolt-to-come will never happen.
The future weaves a different weave.
Future tapestry has a more troublesome pattern.
Remember! In war time, instead of toys there's pain.
My left leg strains
and when the sole touches the ground
bracken in the hedge tickles calve and shin.
I have only to bring my right leg from the tree,
bring it down, to be back in the normal realm again.
I start to do it.
But my right leg doesn't disentangle—

it stays
stuck out at an angle,
will not go down,
with determination remains.

Something has happened to progress.
I clutch at the ivy.
Something has happened to motion.
The leg stays static, apart from my body.
Is it myself or the leg that's contrary,
loose yet strained?
My hand goes under the leg
(I am young enough for short pants)
to puzzle out this inertia—
Why?

What's happened is this:
in the middle of the hedge
an elder sapling
three inches round
has been cut down,
and its end,
shaved to the point of an arrow,
is primed for penetration
of the under-flesh
of my young boy's thigh.

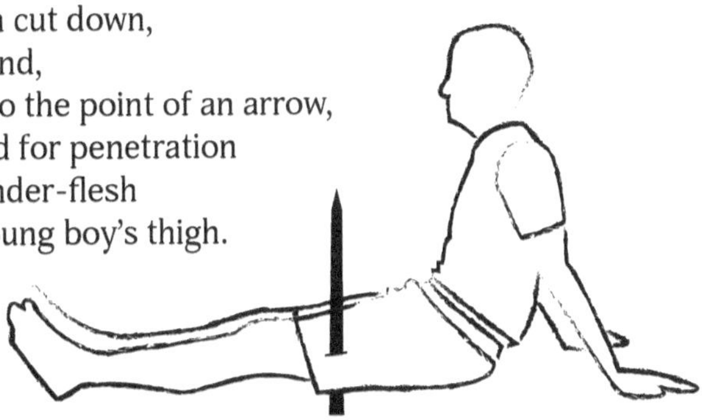

My hand comes back with leaves, clotted red.
I try to grasp the idea of this penetration,
to understand my putty flesh is wounded,
but am confounded there's been no sensation
—MAM!—

though I know that I'm impaled.
                                    —MAM! —
It is my boy soprano.
(I have a good singing voice.)
                                —MAM!! —
My voice is astonished at the hole in my flesh,
forged with no pain.
                            —MAM!!!! —
I've shrieked like this from the front garden
at the attack of the snail, at the snaky worm,
at the appearance of stark wild flowers
in the paddock beyond that garden
                                    —MAM!

THERE ARE FLOWERS!—
flowers more sudden than an appearance
by any wild animal.
                    "MAM!" I scream.

So it's a wonder Mam takes me seriously.
But our back door opens quickly—
"Easy now. Easy."
Facing into Dai Evans meadow,
I believe it is she that is holding me.
                                    "Brave guy."
Thought circumstances
seem to have given her a new *timbre,*
a different vocabulary,
so as not to cause alarm.

On the meadow-side of me,
the hides of the milking cows are solid white
with puddles.
The color of the puddles?
Dark ink and nature green.
Their udders are full because they've been paid a visit

by the bull.
The bull is brought, walking
from Llanwenarth in the night.
Hector and his father,
each holding the end of a different rope
attached to the Bull's head,
lead him through the village to their farm near the church.
Near the graveyard, the bull has a stall to one side.

Bull looks in
over the graveyard
to the field where the lady cows await his visit,
for he's here to put his dongy-dongy into their insides.
If a lady cow wants a calf,
then Bull leaves his dongy-dongy in for a long time.
If it is merely a matter of milk,
his dongy-dongy just tickles her membrane—
the membrane is the brain-part of the belly
and tickling the membrane causes an excitement
that produces milk,
milked into buckets by Jack Evans
in the cow-afternoon at 6 o'clock.

All the while, on the street-side of me,
my Mam is watching—
which proves that the hands,
(one
at the end of the arm coming round me,
the other
showing its pale nails as it appears from the underside
of my mess of a young boy's leg)
are long hands
on the long arms
of a body
viewing my predicament at a close distance.

Close distance is loving.
Long distance is mean.

As the force in the hands struggles
to raise me from the stick,
my head lolls first to the left
where cows in the meadow know what is happening,
then lolls to the right
past Mam, past the hedge, to the street,
to the mountain-stone wall of Dai Evans' market garden.
But both cows and mountain-stone fade—
till in the middle of being carried to the house
a voice that *couldn't* be Mam's tells me:
"I'm carrying you around
because you're the King."

"Let me take him. There's blood on your uniform."
"No, leave him to me." Searching upward,
upward searching,
first his smile, sharp as the lines of his nails,
his smile a glowing patch in his overall blackness.
He is forged from blackness.
His blackness is tenacity.
Tenacity is the all-over flavor
when I linger around his black eyes black forehead
black nose black chin.

He carries me along the path between the currant bushes
through the back door and into the kitchen.
He lays me face-down on the table.
My injury takes up
the entire house—
yet leaves room for him.

Mam is fetching a bucket of water

but not from the well at the bottom of our front garden.
She must be going to the street tap
because I hear the thud of the street gate.

From the cupboard under the stairs,
the Black Man carries towel and sheets.
At the table,
he takes off my shoes—
my tabled shoes are his meal,
he is in a familiar place.

"Do you go to school fella?"
He puts his hands underneath my stomach,
undoing my trousers, my trousers are tearing.
"You're going to have plenty to tell your friends!"

The arrow of the sapling has entered my heart!
I lie skewered,
a pig killed by the pig-killer who lives up the lane.
Convergence of the banks
makes his lane more like an alley.
The pig-killer is a hairy slaughterer who knows death.

I know death!
Uncle Ronnie, killed in a plane crash!
Trevor Williams, 14-year-old son of the school cook
drowned in the river
even as his birthday was celebrated
by the family on the bank!
My Grandmother
trying to talk, but weeping,
not leaving her chair to get a closer look at the coffin.
To get to the church,
the fine black hearse passed her house.
And there was Mrs. Williams

(Trevor's mother)
led through the village,
away from the river
in the Valley of the Shadow.

"Hey, they were my new trousers!"
"We'll get you others!"
"We've got no money!"
"I got money."
"You've got money?!"
"Go tell your friends you got a buddy with lots of money."
"How much?"
He made up a number,
told me to keep it to myself.

Mam carries the grey bucket of water into the kitchen,
having lugged it all along the flagstoned path.
Flagstones in the kitchen, same color as the bucket,
peep from under Mam's home-made mat—
stitched together from left-over scraps of carpet
filched from Mrs. Colonel Probert's,
where she works
taking care of the children,
on the main road, beyond the railway station,
a farm residence, rich and smart.

"How is he?"
"Fine. He's gonna take a ride in an ambulance.
—Ever been in ambulance fella?"
"Nope."
"You'll be carried out on a stretcher
and driven away, lights flashing."
"I must go and phone," Mam says.
He says, "Where you phoning?"
"Up at the post office. It's on the Main Road,

just past the *King of Prussia*.”
“What’s that? The pub?
Why don’t you just phone from there?”
She hesitates.
“Too many people about.”

The black soldier stands.
He’s wrapped one of our ragged towels around his middle
to protect his uniform from what spills.
His hands are hanging.
But his head doesn’t hang—
there come moments when it rises from out his neck
and his neck rises from his back
and his hair might be painted on
except I watch it growing—without moving,
stock still put.

“Old Ma Rodgers will want her husband
to give me a lift back,” Mam tells him.
“Old Ma Rodgers?”
“Old Ma Rodgers works at the post office.”
I explain: “Old Man Rodgers,
he’s got a motor-bike with side-car.
He lets his wife use it.
When he works in the fields
he uses a horse-and-cart and takes cold tea.”
“Cold tea?”
“Yeah.”
“Is it sugared?”
“I didn’t taste it.
But *he* drank it. From his bottle.
I went with him last summer,
him, his horse, his cart, and me.”

“His old bike makes a hell of a noise,” says Mam.

"You'll hear it stop outside the back gate.
When you hear it, run out the front."
"Why?" I ask.
"Because he's a soldier. If he's found here,
he'll get into a lot of trouble at the camp."
"How's he going to get out the front door?"
(The front door was forever locked.)
"I'll tell him where we keep the key."
"You said we weren't to tell nobody!"
"Well, I'll tell *him*," she snaps.

She walks across to me.
Behind her,
ugly men in tall hats
pretty women in long dresses
on the wall paper
separating the back kitchen
from the front room,
singing chorally:
> *Give him the key. Let him have the key.*

"But what if it's only Old Ma Rodgers?" I ask.
"*She* could ride the bike over."
"Uncle Hank will get into trouble whoever it is."
"Uncle who?'
"Uncle Hank," said the soldier.
"And what's your name fella?"
I tell him,
          "Wolf."
Mam says, "It's not. It's Timothy Wilfred. Same as his Dad."
"Wolf is short for Wilfred. And why bring my Dad into it?
I only know him from a photograph."
"It's Tim, nobody calls you Wolf."

Oh, but they did!

12

My Nan and Grandad
(my Dad's Mam and Dad)
who lived in the town,
they'd call me Wolf!
When we'd visit,
to enter their house I had to pass their window—
"Look who's here, my Little Wolfy!" my Nan would shout.

"Keep your strength," says Uncle Hank.
"You'll need it for your ride to the hospital."
For such a real man he was worrying too much.
"What are they going to do?"
"Just give you stitches."
"What does my leg look like? Is my blood running out?"

Mam, close up, next to me, says nothing.
Just like when Uncle Ronnie's coffin
was being transported
she'd said nothing.
Life without him was going to be life without him.
Though when the telegram had arrived
to say he'd died
she'd run from the house round the village,
no shoes, no stockings on her feet.

She goes to the cupboard alongside the grate,
gets a glass to fill with water
from the wide earthenware pot near the window
behind the sink.
He takes it from her as she explains
that to get the front door key
he has to go out the back to the privy
where the key is kept on a ledge under the seat.

He helps me to sit up, to sip the water,

as her brown court shoes
clip-clip over the flagstones.
A new Black Uncle is helping.
While Mam is going to telephone.
This is lucidity.
Except that once she's outside the gate,
lucidity vanishes.
With the sound of her not in front of me
this is a different place.

"Eh, Wolfy!" says the new Black Uncle,
pouring water from the bucket into a white enamel bowl,
"are you afraid to be left alone with this old black guy?"
"I've seen black guys before."
"Naw—"
"Yeah, they frightened a woman."
"What happened?"
"Nothing. They just bought some fish-and-chips."
"Where?"
"The fish-and-chips shop in Rhys."

As he poured water it slopped over into the sink.
This was waste,
but from the point of view of mess it didn't matter—
cos though they wouldn't put in a tap,
we had a drain which ran waste water
through a hole in our wall
down a metal trough
and along to the street.

"Did the black guys sit down in the fish-and-chip shop?"
"No, they went out."
"How old were they?"
"They were like yourself."
"Where did they eat the fish-and-chips?"

"In the town as they walked about."
"Did they have a jeep?"

I don't know—
any more than I know if he has one.
From up in the tree I hadn't seen him,
neither in jeep or bike or lorry
or on his feet.

I *had* seen Old Man Rodgers. And I'd seen the post office.
And Hector, the only young man left in the village.
Also, I think I saw the home guard—old men,
practicing maneuvers,
crawling so the Germans wouldn't see.

"What does my leg look like? Is there blood?"
"Naw!"
"Then why are you wiping it?"
"So's no dirt will get in."
"Is there a big hole?"
"You've got a bit of a gash.
And I'll tell you something, fella—"
he put the fingers of both hands
under the tops of my trousers,
"I'll tell you something—
you're wearing a hell of a pair of shorts."

"They're my underpants."
"What are they made of?"
"A parachute.
My Mam made them.
They're silk. From my Uncle Ronnie's parachute.
He came home once and should have had more leave
but he had to go back for an emergency
and it was a shame cos when he went up in his plane,

it crashed.”

“Parachute silk.”
His voice is imitating the material,
coarse yet silky,
loves to be touched.

“There was any amount of material,
enough to make me trousers and a shirt.”
“A suit!”
“And still material left over enough to make Mam a skirt.”
“*I’ve* got a suit,” boasted my Black Uncle.
“You don’t need a suit. You’ve got your uniform.”
“I mean back home.
You gotta come over and visit.
You can wear your parachute suit and I’ll wear mine.”
“No, my parachute shirt-and-trousers is *not* a suit.
I got a suit though. It’s my Uncle Ronnie’s.
It’s no good for me now.
In a couple of years, My Gran says, it’ll fit me fine.”

“Naw! I want you to wear your parachute.
For me, it’s a suit.
Tell me what your friends said
when they saw you all dolled up!”

“I only wore it once.”
“Who saw you?”
“My Nan and Grandad in the town
and the women waiting for the bus.
My Nan said, “Look who’s here. All dressed up.”
“And the women at the bus?”
“They all said I looked smart.”

Talking can hurt.

The hurt of fingers caught in a door.
One finger five fingers twenty.
Impossible to say how many.
More and many are not the same.

"Is it hurting fella?"
This Black Uncle's hand
is on the top of my leg.
As the fingers of hurt climb
up the walls of the wound,
his black hand
is color in a hurtless area.
I half sit up. I hold to his hand.

"It hurts to get better," he assures me.
To empty the enamel bowl full of my blood
he crosses to the sink.
"When it's hurting, it's mending."
His voice is so intimate
across the distance of the kitchen—
what's his trick?

"When you wear *your* suit,
what do *your* friends say?" I ask.
"They like it. Got to be careful though—"
"Why?"
"—of folks who are jealous
to see this black guy struttin'."

"I've got nasty friends too.
When my Gran comes past the school
to speak through the railings
they come up and pretend they like me."
"You must have a best friend though?"
"Trevor Watkins

who was drowned in the river—
sometimes I liked him."
"Sometimes?"
"Well, when we had a party at the hut ground,
he took home *all* the prizes."
"Well, why didn't you win?
You gotta learn to play games, fella!"
He presses my eyes with a piece of the torn sheet.

"And you gotta learn to climb."
"I can climb!"
"If you can climb, why are you lying here sniveling?"
Unfairness
causes tears to spout from all parts of my face.
He presses my forehead,
lifts my chin.

He puts the bowl in the sink, then opens the back door
into the darkening half-dark night.
"I'm going to relieve myself . Do you need to?"
"No."
Though I would love to see his dicky.
How black would be his dicky? In the night,
I'd have to touch it
cos I couldn't see.

And when I wanted to,
how *would* I relieve myself?
All the people who ever lived were piddlers.
Will I be able to piddle lying down?

Daphne Jenkins, my young teacher
who teaches in the young classroom,
piddle-dee-widdles in the girls' toilet.
The toilet, built of the same red brick as the school,

gives the school building a nice finish-off.
In the school toilet she doesn't have
to worry about burying her activity.
School toilet is a proper toilet,
water comes when you pull a chain.

Oppy Pritchard, headmistress,
does her widdling beside the school
in her private house.
Like the rest of life, her widdling
has to be at a distance—
or God will glower.
Her lameness must make it an ordeal,
discomfortable as remembering
the names of nations
or gaging the speed of a hedgehog
at so-and-so many miles an hour.

In summer,
Hector pisss right in the fields where he works—
the stream coming out of him as clear
as the unshirted upper body of him.
But after his bottle of cold tea
the wee-wee-pee of Old Man Rodgers comes slow
on the railway line,
expressing the possibility of being run over by a train.

Best of all,
past Gran's house
down Church Lane
a soldier had been buttoning up
after his piddledeepissing.

An American jeep
parked inside the gate to a small wood

had been the hint.
In this wood a brook runs in a gulley,
with blue-bells and trees growing on its slopes.
From the top of the bank of the gulley
there's a long view of the brook
to where it crosses a field as it leaves the wood.
In the field a horse watches the water and considers
pissing a piss then stamping a stamp.
The young American soldier atop the opposite bank
is buttoning up his fly
until there are no more buttons
because of his belt.

He comes down the bank
crossing the brook
and as he comes up my side
(the trees being too slender
to hide behind)
I lie down among the blue-bells
their stems sucking into sweet moist earth
where their roots mingle
with grass roots with tree roots with weed roots—
which in this underneath are not considered weeds.

As the soldier lopes past
little can I ascertain
tallness or shortness
though, damn, I enjoy his freckles!
And the singeing of pissed-on roots
is the texture of the air.

There's no way of knowing
if he knows I'm watching,
if he enjoys being watched on the sly.

He opens the gate
gets in the jeep
drives out
gets out the jeep
closes the gate
drives off.

I lie where I am
looking across to where he's peed,
to where the jeep has been parked.
I am as old as nature.
Young as the bluebells.
Sweet as the grass.

"How you feeling Wolfy? Finished hollering?"
My Black Uncle had been too full of pee
to have peed in the privy.
He must have gone into the front garden
to pee under the apple tree that produces no apples—
gazing out to the railway line
beyond the stream coming out of him,
splashing the bark
(the underneath of the bark smells of lavender)
drenching the moss.

He strokes my leg,
then takes a chair
from the side of the table to the head.
Sits.
As the chair rears up,
he balances back—
considers into me.
He reminds me of Old Man Rodgers
in his cart
considering the guiding of his horse.

"Don't fall asleep, fella!
You sleep, and your leg'll drop off!"
"I'm not," I murmur.
To catch what I am saying he leans forward.
My chin rests on the pads near his wrists.
I realize my cheeks are between the palms
of my Black Uncle's hands.

"You'd better light the lights," I tell him.
"We've got two lamps."

"You just tell this old guy what you want, fella!
What do you want most of all?
Do you want to come with me to America?"
"I...I want to go to Porthcawl."

This is where Kids and Mams and Dads went
before Hitler.
If there's no money for fish-and-chips
it's alright to take sandwiches,
providing you eat them a good hour
before you go on the *Caterpillar*.
Otherwise, you'll be sick.

"Where's Porthcawl?"
"It's at the seaside.
You've got to go through a railway tunnel."
"I'll take you."
"You can't."
"Why?"
"It's closed because of the war."

"Well—"
He refills the tumbler
from the earthenware pot beside the sink.

"Ever been in a car fella?"

"Nope."
"When I was your age
I'd never been in a car neither.
If we can't go to Porthcawl,
I'll take you somewhere else."

"Is your car here?"
"Not at the moment—
you've got your choice of truck or jeep."

Then, quietly,
he takes me on a journey.
I have to go
cos beggars can't be choosey.
But then again
I'm no beggar,
and still he's taking me.
Oh! in truck or jeep
he's driving me
in a matter of minutes into Rhys
on into the mountains
where we visit castles.
But let it be understood—
of this ride no one knows nothing
nothing at all about this afternoon.
What a soldier does is kept secret.
People who let the secret out are spies.

But *not* to tell
could also be telling lies, akin in shame
to when I'd picked the daffodils
from the churchyard
to be sold in bunches—

one to Mrs Reynolds
who has a deaf daughter up the alley
(an alley is a street too narrow to be a street),
two to Mrs. Irish Pat, one to Hector's Mam.
All tied up with string at three pence.
I say they've come from our own garden,
arranged in their own leaves.

Mam is all curiosity when she finds the money,
then goes looney and forces me to explain.
She puts the money in an envelope.
I have to take it to Doctor Corner in his rectory,
and I am to tell him:
                    "I'll never steal flowers
                    from a graveyard
                    throughout the rest of my real life."
"What you did was shameful."
Doctor Corner explains
that a psalm-a-day will be good for me.
A psalm-a-day is what I should read.
He gives me a purple bible, a small one,
taken down from a high overladen place.

"The only one I'll tell about you, is my Dad,"
I assure Uncle Hank,
convinced that the mitigation for deceit
is a drop of honesty with someone close.
He tips my chin to bring water to my lips,
leans back, takes a sip himself.
I'd tell him about the dangers of sharing—
except that I like his lips being where my lips have been
and where my lips will be again.

Dim light of the early night
hits the brass knob and brass finger-shield

of the door ever-open to the front room.
"My Dad's got a jeep. Mam's got a photo."
"Is he driving?"
"He's sitting in a seat."
"Where is he?"
"Egypt."

Egypt separates out from my injury.
Oh, the exhaustion of distinguishing what something is
from its name!

Uncle Hank is sitting on the bottom step of the stairs
in the shadows.
Can't see his face.
Might be wearing a gas mask.
His low chin is the mask's lower chamber
where occurs
the separation of gas from air from pain.

"Egypt's abroad."
"I shouldn't think your Dad's trouble.
If he's your Dad, he must be a wolf just like yourself."
"He's a man."
"Ever seen him?"
"Mam saw him last year, at the pictures, in the news,
 in a tank."
"Think she might be mistaken?"
"No. She went back.
My Gran came to look after me.
Mam saw him two times—

—where are you going."
"Upstairs to get the lamp."

His feet are quiet.

He's taken his shoes off.
Also, there'd been enough
of Mrs. Colonel Probert's left-over carpet
to make pads for the stairs.

Deep in the wallpaper
I see Dad
among the gents and ladies.
Then I get tired, I get older,
and as I look at the wall paper
Dad leaves—
though ladies and gents remain,
ladies free, men leaning
in copycat positions
on their canes
around a house
with six facade pillars
caging an interior
bigger than my house and garden
by a thousand times.

Do Dad and the men in the wallpaper
have interiors big as that house,
big as Oppy Prichard's voice?

Oh!
Is that my Black Uncle
coming back down the stairs?
He's probably on the landing
where I'd been with Gran
that afternoon we got up from Mam's bed
after we'd been fast asleeping.
Us on the landing,
Mam on the stairs
three steps from the bottom

reading the telegram about Uncle Ronnie
killed in the plane crash—
the telegram beginning:
                    WE REGRET TO INFORM...

Footsteps now around Mam's big bed.
And clumping on the bare floor—
for Mam decided to use up the last of the left-over carpet
not for the bedroom upstairs
but for a big mat downstairs in the front room.

Footsteps.
I didn't hear the abrasion of the match
but he must have lit the lamp
for he lets out a shout.
"Damn! You've bled all over my uniform!"
Down the stairs he comes
with lamp flickering.
It's a lamp to be held at the top
and walked about.

"You!" he's exclaiming
as he comes back into the back kitchen
with a sidelong glance at me,
"You!"

Below the waist-level of him
the lamp light is moving.

A shadow of me
on the table
on the wall—
or is it the ladies with the gents moving?
Who was the thinker,
who made the positions on the wall-paper?

27

If I knew the thinker,
would I understand the thought?

Glows
from weak shafts of light
topple in timid tracks
along floor wall ceiling
of the back kitchen
as Uncle Hank takes the small hand-lamp
into the front room.

There, the oak central table
is heavy enough
to harbor within it
degrees of shine.
Underneath,
four thick legs
joined by a criss-cross of planks
make four compartments
to be sat in when the Gerries come over—
always me, sometimes Gran,
but never Mam.
With the planes overhead,
Mam will go out in the garden.
When the German pilots see her, because she's lovely,
they do their killing further on.

Now he brings the lamp back, holds it up.
"Come on, Fella."
He tries to raise my head.
"What are you doing to my leg." I whine. "Stop pinching."
"You feel that?"
"Stop pinching!"
"Who's pinching. I'm rubbing.
Honest to God, fella, you can't stand nothing.

If I was your Dad
I'd throw you up,
wouldn't try to catch you,
let you disappear into the ground."

Couped down at table's head—
black face of black man close to white kid's white face.

Drink your water. Are you hungry?"
"—Dunno."
"Boy, am I going to get into trouble!
What with you telling your Dad.
Then you messing up my uniform."
"What'll they do?"
"Lock me up.
Give me bread and water.
Hey! You must not sleep!
Stop dropping off. You need food."

Black Uncle carrying lamp over to cupboard
near window and earthenware pot.
Sides & top of cupboard are mesh,
bottom & frame of cupboard are wood.
I believe
I can see through the mesh but can't.
Cupboard is what Mam calls it.
Cooling box is what Gran calls it.

"There's nothing in here but lard."
"What's lard?"
"Meat fat."
"You're talking about drippings."
"Drippings!!"
He shifts the lamp to light inside the cooling box,
to see if there is something hiding.

"Yup, drippings is all you got.
What did you eat today, Fella?"
"I had apples, and some bread and milk."

With no food around
all he can do is refill the tumbler with water,
bring it across to me.
He is adjusting into a different stance.
"Where are you going now?"
"Into the front room to light another lamp.
I need more light, to get clean."

We keep the largest lamp
on the sideboard in the front room.
To be able to see where he is going,
he takes the small lamp with him
leaving me in gloom—
and as he puts it down on the sideboard
to free his hands,
the small flame gives a roar as it bulbs up.
Though I can't see,
the front of him must be aglare
while the back of him must be a shadow.

On the large lamp there's a frosted glass globe
around the glass funnel.
As he removes them, they chink,
and the muscles of his shoulders under his shirt
execute accidental moves that comply.
A determined move is his striking of the match
to light the lamp.
The front room will stay lit now,
for I know there's enough paraffin
and enough wick to take the flame.

Glass funnel and frosted glass globe are replaced.
I'm in the dark back kitchen,
but I know light is falling
on the front room sideboard,
on the central table,
on the old stone fireplace,
on Mam's home-made mats,
on armchairs that look like brown parchment,
and on the mirror above the fireplace
with its corner crack
creating a corner within the mirror
imaging other-dimensionally—
its surface readied for this soldier's skin,
his face.

With delicacy
he attaches a cover to the funnel.
This cover is a doll's umbrella
protecting our ceiling from the soot
that Gran claims is invisibly floating.
Gran has a lamp cover
and got this one for Mam.
Sometimes Mam uses it.
Sometimes not.

Its silver metal stem is finer than one of Mam's hair pins,
divided at the bottom by a cut
so that it can slide on
and then hold steady
to the rim of the glass funnel,
supporting the top of the umbrella
to which it is joined forever, two inches above.
This umbrella, big as a half-crown coin,
is divided into panes.
The frames of the panes are doll's matchsticks.

The umbrella had been white,
the doll's matchsticks had been ivory.
Now, from heat and smoke they're an oil-colored musk.
Yet the previous ivory is more than a memory
for it matches now the cream of his palms.
The dark arm of him
angling to adjust the tiny umbrella
is a muscular activity bequeathed to the village—
in front of him he has created
a front room new and strong and kind.

Finished,
he returns the smaller light into the back kitchen,
placing it down at the hearth.
This light from the hearth is *his* shine—
readying for an escape.
An escape is the end of his visit.
He might not come back.
He smooths my leg, bends down
to lightly kiss my cheek.

Best place to tidy himself up
is before the tiny mirror
on the window-sill near the earthenware pot.
Looking at himself in that tiny mirror
with the low light from the small lamp
barely reaching—
he undoes the buttons of his shirt.

"Uncle Hank."
"What do you want, Fella?"
"You've forgotten the blackout!"
"Damn!"
He pulls down the black-out shade
on the back kitchen window,

then runs into the front room to do the same.
As he runs his skin is black with purple in it.
I can see because, as he runs, he takes off his shirt.

I tell him:
"If Mam thinks there are going to be bombers
she looks at the front door to see if the holes are stuffed."
He goes over to see if there are any gaps
in the felt strips Mam has nailed around
to prevent spillage.
"Sometimes she takes the doormat from the back door
and puts it along the bottom of the door in there.
She says if there's no draft coming in,
no light can get out."

"Damn! You're making this old guy work.
But I don't mind. You know why?"
He leans on the table, eyes dropping deep into me.
"I don't mind because you're smart!"

Daphne Jenkins, my teacher,
once told me the same
when she congratulated me on knowing
that rather than ten 49s listed down the page
it was better to multiply 49 x 10.

Memories of congratulation
don't prevent me from taking in
that in a village without young men,
this black man is only the second man
I've seen shirtless.

First man without his shirt was Hector,
only-son of the farmer
with the fields down by the river.

To prevent their dying,
sons of farmers
are not allowed to go to war.
This sole young man
wants to impress
that he's fully grown.
He's mowing the field
opposite the bus-stop
and though his tractor can be heard
neither he nor the tractor can be seen.
Luckily the bus comes late
so we don't miss him—
for suddenly above the hedge on the high bank
we see him
without his shirt
fresh as the burdocks
that sprout to small tree size.
"Don't encourage him," says Mrs. Irish Pat.
"It's not that hot. He's showing off.
I'm not looking," she insists, "I'm looking for the bus.
He's already mowed that part five times."

Pain in my leg
throbs through the walls of the wound,
pain throbs through the village,
pain throbs through the world.
Uncle Hank appears in his underpants,
carrying his uniform
into the pain of the back kitchen
from the pain of the stairs.

He gets the small lamp from the hearth
and takes it over to the window-sill
By its light, on the table near the sink,
he sponges his shirt and trousers.

Water from the earthenware pot
is only to be used for drinking,
but I don't tell him this—
for the shine on his nakedness
gives him license to project influence
through the drain
onto the village,
onto Doctor Corner
in gaiters and frock coat
longing to be a bishop
(Doctor Corner who has a brother fresh out of prison)
(fresh out, again);
onto Hector who, passing on his bike,
causes flowers to open;
onto Old Man Rodgers whose cold tea
gives him strength to tauten the wire fence
between the wooden posts
just past the level crossing
up at the station
where there are few trains from Cardiff
but plenty of stations in between.

Uncle Hank is positioning himself
to fulfill the violent purpose of his soldier life.
Violence is German bombers coming over.
Nearby, they dropped a bomb.
The bomb didn't explode, so all we've known is peace.

"I've got to pop back upstairs to get my tie.
Are you looking forward to your trip in the ambulance?
You'll be out and about in the middle of the night!"

"I won't tell my Dad you've been here," I cried out
with a sound that was my body,
not my voice.

Uncle Hank comes over, lies on the table,
horizontally cradles,
calls me *a good fella*,
strokes my hair.

But no sooner does he lie down,
than he goes upstairs to fetch his tie—

which is to say
he takes away
the arms attached
to the upper part of him and me.

"Uncle Hank, don't take the lamp
into the front bedroom
until you've pulled down the blind.
Don't forget to pull the curtains
across the landing window."

Is he in the bedroom?
Or is he standing on the landing,
looking at the mounds of lady cows in the dark fields,
at the dark church
where once every Sunday morning
and once every Sunday afternoon
Oppy Pritchard's contralto voice sings hymns
to the invisible day-time moon.

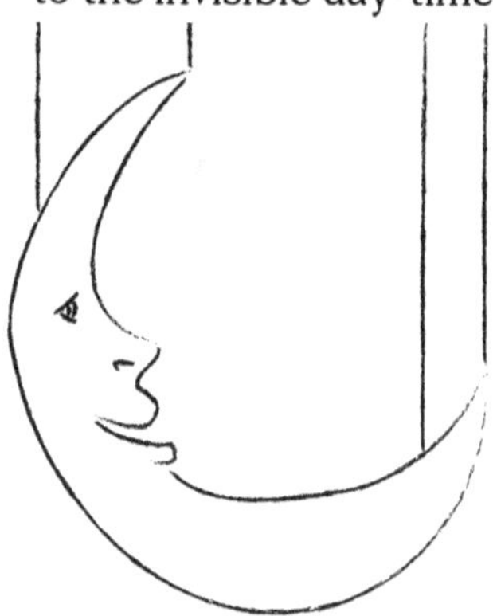

MAM

They carried Timmy out
to the buckled bent-up ambulance.
With doors open and engine humming
it was similar to a military vehicle—
though, out here in the country, it was peripheral to war.
Ernie Wilson, driver,
and Gus Baron, his assistant,
used to live up the lane opposite *The King of Prussia*.
Paid next to nothing
as farm laborers—
they tended gardens for a bit of extra cash.

Living next door to each other
among the overgrown,
there was 'speculation'
concerning their leaving
not an atom of time
for anyone except each other.
So, they moved into Rhys.

A good move.
With the war at full throttle,
they were less talked-of.
Also, they got jobs at the *secret* Ammunitions Dump.

This Dump was a giant mound covered with grass
in the midst of uninhabited country.
We were supposed to think it was a mountain.
Clod earth on clod earth.
How could that be—?
There were guarded gates,
and a drive leading up to vast doors
cut deep into the mountain.
What were we supposed to think was beyond those doors?
Woolworths?

It's still there, grass better cut,
drive and doors well cared for.
Wars end. Wars begin.
At this anti-place
somebody believes
in the dire necessity of carrying on.

The Rules—.
Don't ask why Ernie and Gus
have double the money.
Don't ask about the little green bus
that stops near the Asylum
and takes workers to nowhere .
Believe—.
Gus and Ernie's work was solely ambulance work,
though war kept civilians healthy here in the country.
Death occurred only in large cities, in large towns.

Anyway, Gus and Ernie were *not* conscripted.
Reasons could've be religious
(they might've been Quakers
with their nature of belonging to themselves).

They *did* belong to themselves.
After we won the war, they managed the town cinema.
Along the way they both acquired wives.
At some uncertain point the wives died.

Through the village, Ernie was *not* driving smoothly.
Side-roads were in poor condition
and there had been little concentration
on the idea of seat-springs.
Later in the century, there are cars like boats,
buses like ships.
Mesmerized villagers later learn

to sail down country lanes.

Once on the main road, travelling was easier,
for the surface had to be taut for convoys.
Still, travel was slow in the late evening/early night,
for headlights had only the strength of flashlights,
their hooded beams directed at the immediate ground.

"Nothing to worry about,"
shouted Ernie back over his own head,
"we'll be there in a jiffy."
But the planes were so close we could hardly hear him.
They might have been coming to kiss us
in the woods
along the lanes.

We pulled up to the curb,
hiding beneath the branches of an overwhelming tree.
On the left,
we were just past the railway station.
On the right,
we were just before the drive to Mrs. Colonel Probert's,
which is where I worked.
Beyond Ernie's head, through the windscreen,
appeared a rabbit.
This paddock, on all sides wooded,
belonged to Mrs. Colonel Probert
and was full of rabbits cursed with short lives.
A way out of the general predicament
was to be shot in the heart,
put in a stew, and shatted out.
This particular rabbit, singly, on its hind legs,
was a lesson in boldness
plunged out of darkness
plunged out of quietness
by our headlights

and by the planes.

"He just went off then, did he?"
Ernie was talking about Hank.
I'd told them I'd had help from a black soldier
who happened to be passing.
"No idea as to the soldier's name?"

—If Timmy remembered Hank when he woke up,
I'd meet the moment by asking Gus,
"Why do you tie your raincoat belt so tight?
Is it to remind Ernie of your tiny waist?"
My method was to knock gossip deep in the mire
before another question escaped.

"He didn't want no *thank-yous*?"
"No. He carried Timmy into the house
and went off without a by-your-leave."
"They're strong," said Gus,
coming to sit next to me on the cot across from Tim.
"Yeah, and they've got good hearts."
This conversation had as much to do
with implications of the sultry,
as it had to do with Hank.
"Treat them right and they'll treat you right,"
Ernie whispered over his shoulder.
"They're just like everybody else."
I said, "It was good of him to help.
Timmy might have died."
"Who wouldn't help a woman as pretty as yourself—
they love white women.
They got this monstrous equipment between the legs.
And when they get started, they can't stop."
I grinned, because not to grin
would only have encouraged Gus's smut.

"Gus!" remonstrated Ernie.
"Mrs. Tyler doesn't want to know anything about that."
"I'm not saying nothing that shouldn't be said.
We don't want our women getting hurt, that's all."

The sound of the planes had lessened.
"They aren't Gerries, " said Ernie,
"they're ours, looking for Gerries.
We've been told they're expecting an attack on the Dump."
"I'm glad we don't work there," he added.
"I'll say," said Gus.

Ernie considered it safe now to re-start the engine,
so again we were off to the hospital
in an ambulance full of proclamations
concerning dimensions and fertilization and lust.

Hank *is* formed well enough
and when we learned what others expected
we enjoyed shared amusement, shared shock.
First off, he was shy.
Undressing so close up to me,
I was able to see nothing.
To get a good look
every time he took off his clothes, I'd move back.
And realizing just what I was doing,
he go to the other extreme.
Oh, if I had friends,
I'd have loved them to watch him parading.
His parading was serious play.

Me? I'm modest.
In my heart I used to be . . .
At the beginning, going out with my husband, Wilfred,
I was afraid to tell him when I needed to pee.

But with Hank, I became so advanced,
one day I didn't wear underclothes.
As I lifted my dress up, and up,
he got so much pleasure he had to go me one better
and he ran out the door naked, saying,
"I'll be back in two minutes."
He returned an hour later,
claimed in the night there was no one to see him
and if they did, it was his outline only
cos his blackness was blacker than the dark.

"You can't say that," I warned him.
Lah-di-das don't sleep at night
cos they sit on their bums all day.
Doctor Corner the parson,
head full of sermons, belly full of wine,
might get up from bed and go out into the fields.
If he made out a naked black man,
he'd never return to my house to have our little talks.
He'd come to the door, knock too strongly,
to suggest he was God.
I'd already told him straight I couldn't believe in a God
that allowed young men to die on the battlefield,
couldn't believe in a God
that allowed my lovely young brother to die in his plane.
He mumbled—
something about this being Man's fault not God's,
nor *his* nor *mine*.

After my divorce scandal he never came to talk anyway.
If I'd known my divorce was going to happen
I would have told Hank to go out stitch-stark
whenever he was so inclined.
I would have said,
"Take a bucket,

water from the tap at the stone beside the street
wants to run in the crevice between your buttocks.
The crevice between your buttocks
is a respite from the acreage of your black ass."
"Who told you the water likes my crevice?"
"Water. Water thinks.
Water talks."

But then
certain moments
we needed to be quieter.
Quieter is sane.

Now I'm old.
I go to the mirror,
arrange strips and wisps of my white hair.
I pull myself together
for all the others.
These days I don't see them...
These days I'm blind...

In the war days
with my hair in a roll
I'd go into town and walk around.
I'd ask the butcher, "Well, Mr. Price, what have you got?"
"Strips of shredded pork, Mrs. Tyler."
"Let me have a look," I'd say.
"What do you reckon?"
"Oh, Mr. Price," I'd say,
"I could *never* think of anything to do with *that*."
I'd use the accent of Mrs. Colonel Probert,
causing the town to believe me a toff.
My hair was rolled round an elastic band
when there was one available.
When there wasn't, I'd go out with my hair falling,

the naturalness of its wave pronounced.
Mrs. Colonel Probert had nice hair
and if the news said *no air raids expected*
she'd go into Cardiff and have it bobbed.
She knew how to walk. She knew how to stop.
When she stopped
her muscles took a breath.
When she was tired, her muscles sobbed.

Tantalizing to watch her
in her garden, stooping down to cut parsley,
or in the kitchen instructing the cook.
She, herself, was going to prepare lunch for the children—
boiled eggs and parsley sauce.
When it was prepared,
she leaned across the nursery table to serve them.
Her leaning
was elegant
as the ornate plaster ceiling
built too high to show off its animals.
Her children asked, "What is it that's up there, Mummy?"
Plaster lambs and ravens?
Plaster lambs and doves?

The nursery was one of the smaller rooms
on the ground floor, at the back of the house.
I had to pass by to get to the kitchen,
making sure that from door to door I kept close to the wall
where windows look out onto the cow shit,
a mountain of manure,
and the land girls collecting cans.
Milk cans, full in the dawning,
were returned empty, at dusk.
Servants were instructed never to look at the gentry.
We were never to look into the nursery

where she sat at the table with her children,
opening a letter from her husband who, like Wilfred,
was in North Africa.
Though *she* had no need to be anxious,
her husband was one of the big shots,
his father, an army big shot before him,
his grandfather a big shot before that.
"Big shots come back."

The white five-bar gate, the drive, the house, were lonely,
confident and lonely, as we passed by in the ambulance.
Mrs. Colonel Probert went to bed early.
Asleep, teased by the Sphinx,
she'd be fingering herself in her antique bed,
in her antique house.
The Sphinx was coming over from Egypt,
the Sphinx was of uncertain sex.
So, in her dream, she was adamant—
"Whatever you do, bring along your equipment.
Get to Paddington Station early,
cos there's only one train."

As we got into Rhys,
Ernie was calm, driving without spurts.
No street lamps.
Windows covered with black-outs.
Headlights shielded.
Traffic just wasn't.
(Just a tiny bit of traffic, that is.)

Shapes of mountains, churches, pubs,
of the asylum, of the town hall,
bulked over us.
Yet in the dark, young men loom bright.
Hank lay in a white cloud,

which accentuated his blackness.
Hector sat on a skulking dark cloud
because he was white.
Boys stretched out their arms from the roof tops.
A group of young women were squeezed up in a huddle
down by the river, in front of a cave.
Hank and Hector were in their underpants.
Wartime underpants were made of a material
constructed less to cover up flesh than to contain.
Languid hair covering their calves was a come-on.
Also, the bulge of the crotch,
the large knob of the masculine knee.

Ernie and Gus lay Tim on a stretcher,
then had trouble getting across the gravel to the door
for their flashlights, shielded like the headlights,
gave out only weak little beams.
It was a small cottage hospital.
A single bulb shone in the hall and on the stairs.
But when we got to the room at the back,
three fierce bulbs glared down on the examination table
on which Timmy was laid.
The examination table
the steel trolley
steel kidney bowls
the tops of the medicine bottles
all shone so brightly
you'd have said they had bulbs inside.
This was not a room to contain secrets.

When Timmy recovers,
what will his brain think he believes?
What can it believe that could be presented as evidence?
Hank came over the fields,
then over the stile at the bottom of the garden.

Hedges have grown up and over.
Nothing's overlooked.
There's no one now to tend the overgrown hedges.
The overgrowth stays.

Ernie instructed Gus to drive the ambulance over
to collect my mother-in-law and father-in-law
(Wilfrid's Mam and Dad)
from their house opposite the sweets-factory
that we had in fact already passed on our way to hospital.
In case he could be, in some regard, useful,
Ernie was going to stay close outside, on the porch.
Five minutes without Gus was going to be agony.
I gave him a kiss, slap on his lips, to show thanks.

The nurse on the evening shift
was Mrs. Irish Pat. Timmy knew her.
Mrs. Irish Pat was from the self-same village.
She was a nurse with next-to-no training.
With her husband away fighting,
she wanted to do something.
So, she'd packed herself into a tight white uniform
and tucked her blond hair under a cap.

Mrs. Irish Pat, paying little attention to Timmy,
jawed on about her husband in Burma.
Pulled out a snapshot.
He was outside a temple.
He looked to have rouge on his cheeks.
Ah, Mr. Irish Pat and the temple—
enough jargon to write several bibles.
Words that escaped jargon
were *peace* and *sleep.*

When he came home on leave,

he needed *peace* and *sleep,* but didn't get any.
Mrs. Irish Pat sent him out.
Oh, she might have prepared him a dinner,
but before he could eat it
she'd sent him on the bike to get bread from the shop.
She was friends with a butcher
who gave her extra on her rationing card.
If she heard of something on the black market
she'd send him pedaling into Rhys.
She killed him—.
Just two years after he was demobbed,
he died of a series of heart attacks.

"I can't wait for him to come home.
Wonderful—!! Them over in North Africa.
Protecting the country.
Protecting the family."
She sounded like the radio.
Like Oppy Pritchard, headmistress.
Like a student at the school of rot.

Oppy Pritchard, headmistress,
up at the main road as we were waiting for a bus.
"Sorry to hear about your brother.
Must be a comfort to know he died a hero."
A *hero*?
Brazen idea.
He was a dead eighteen-year-old soldier,
with decomposing body, decomposing face.
Hero. So easily said all over Britain.
Dare say all over Germany.
Must ask Hank if they're saying it in the United States.

"Mam..." Timmy opened his eyes
and straightaway sat up.

"Alright, love? You're here in the cottage hospital
with a hole in your leg cos of an accident up on the bank."
"Where's Uncle Hank?"
"Who?" asked Mrs. Irish Pat.
"A black soldier. He was passing.
Came into the garden and got Timmy off the stick
when he heard him scream."
"—Oh." she said.
"They say there's quite a few of them up at the camp!"

When Doctor David Davis came in
she couldn't wait to talk about the black man.
"The wound could have been messy.
The stick penetrated deeply.
It being so tidy and clean means the black man
had great strength to lift Timmy up and clear,
rather than sliding him off."
They both agreed.
Dr. David Davis,
before and after the war
a horn player in the town's orchestra,
took the subject over.
"...and on top of being strong, they are musical,
they play all kinds of instruments, trained and untrained."

When Wilfred's Mam and Dad came in
David Davis told them, "That black man was a blessing—."
Then went into the description of the passing black man
going up to Timmy on the bank,
after hearing him scream.

Nora, Wilfred's Mam, told us,
"I goes up to market with my friend Veronica
to buy material for curtains
and we walks through the place and right out the back

to where they cut material to measure
from folds bought on the black market in Cardiff
and then transported by cattle truck into Rhys.
Who should be standing on the cattle truck
showing off the folds
but a black man from the colonies."
What colonies? God knows!

Friend Veronica was magnetized.
"I could stand here all day looking."
Curtain material?!
If he was selling sausages,
Veronica wouldn't tear herself away.

As well as himself
and what his name might be,
there was *much more* to consider.
From a roll, he shot the fabric in a great billow,
yards over the heads of the crowd in front of him.
Then whipped it back.
The crowd, confused by a sexual anticipation,
didn't feel altogether sane.

Granpa Dan said, "It's a bloody good job
it's just the material he whipped out."
We laughed! We laughed!
Because this remark needed effort to think of,
and courage to perform—
Granpa Dan was, in fact, exhausted,
so went out into the garden
to have a smoke.

Instead of sewing up the wound,
it was to be opened up a little more,
then filled with tape dipped in disinfectant.

Doctor David Davis asked us to leave
and as I turned to go out—I had a last look.
The wound was white, inside.
The tape was the color of apples lying on the ground.
Oh, the vulnerability of fallen apples.
Of boys with soldier fathers
who have rubbed their children out of mind.

Out on the porch
Granpa Dan and Nora and me and Ernie talked
about how difficult it must have been for Hank
to lever Timmy off the stake.
"He had to be careful so as to cause no further hurt."
"They can be delicate."
"It's that what makes them good fighters."
"And good workers. Have you seen the plantations?
"Especially tobacco. Planted in those neat rows."

Granpa Dan told us, "*I'm* a good worker.
If it wasn't for age, I'd be at the front,
I'd be fighting even at this late stage of life."
Nora whispered,
"I'm just happy to have you home in the house."
When she arrived, she was crackling,
sharing in a situation always made her feel alive—
but Nora was fading now.
"There isn't much we can do here. Timmy's very quiet.
It's a nasty wound. But he'll be alright!"
Ernie offered to get Gus
to take them back in the ambulance.
Gus was out in the garden, by the brook.
But by now the planes had finished flying over to Cardiff,
so Nora told him to leave Gus where he was.
"We'll be able to walk home. Give us a kiss love.
Tell your mother she's always in my mind."

Having mentioned my mother,
Nora wouldn't stay another minute.
She and Granpa Dan had three boys, living—
Wilfred and Fred in the army, Eric in the navy.
Whereas my mother lost her only son (my brother).
And her husband (my father, Timmy's grandfather)
ran away with a one-legged woman.
And her brother was killed
by a sniper in the first World War.
Which meant that every male had been stolen from her.
Except Timmy, her grandson.
He wasn't yet a teenager.
Afraid of losing him, she suffocated him with love.

Ernie gave me a *Woodbine*,
and through the smoke of the cigarettes
night grew:
measures of night
measures of light
where the wind parted the branches for a small moon.
Gus was out there.
We could hear his footsteps when he was on the gravel.
"Gus?" Ernie whispered into the garden,
"do you want a *Woodbine*?"
Gus answered, "I'll be over in a minute.
I enjoy being here in the dark."

It was said that Ernie had nearly bitten off Gus's testicles.
That he got too passionate.
I could see what Ernie saw in Gus.
Gus was so thin he couldn't get any thinner,
and what strands of hair remained
were black and due to last
with no discernible change in sight.
Ernie felt safe for years to come.

Our matches kept going out
but in the end we lit another *Woodbine*
and as we sucked in the smoke
the red dots
were a target for aircraft with their aircraft guns.
The war had gone on so long,
we enjoyed the tempting of just about anything.
We thought we understood our resilience.
We were wrong.

I'm not one to count days and dates.
But I'm confident in saying Hank's baby
was not in me at that time.
He gave me his baby the last time we were together,
that same afternoon Timmy found us in the bedroom
and to get rid of him I said Hank had a thorn in his hand.
"I've got to get it out,
Hank doesn't want anyone watching—
they might cry."
Timmy left.
As soon as he'd gone, I was able to open up
and Hank delved into me
times without number.
After we finished, we lay on the bed
and it was my mother who discovered us
naked as the new day.
Hank was so black
she couldn't speak to him.
It was to me she screamed,
"Tell him to leave! I want him gone!"

I didn't have money to buy a cradle,
so I made one from an old suitcase,
with baby's pillowcases made from towels

and baby's blanket from curtains.
Sick as I was, I couldn't stop getting out of bed
in the course of day and night to look at him.
How small! How he refused to take up space!
How pale he was. How I wished him to be as dark as Hank
in the those few days he was alive.
"This is your little brother," my mother told Timmy.
"God loves him so much,
he's taking him back—
not allowing him to stay."

A couple of months into the pregnancy I was enormous.
I didn't leave the house,
moving my hands and knees,
thinking like a spider going up and down the stairs.
With all young men away,
young pregnant women were unheard of.
And so I pretended Wilfred came home one night
from North Africa.
"Don't tell my Mam and Dad!"
is what I said he said.
I said the combat he was engaged in was so important
his visit had to be kept secret,
the situation so dangerous they allowed him
only one night's leave.

Hank's tiny boy was buried in a tiny wooden coffin
provided by Doctor Corner through some parish charity.
Doctor Corner suggested a good name for a boy
was 'Christopher.'
Christopher comes from Christ,
who might have been the father.
General consensus was against 'Wilfred'.
A journey from Egypt would have tired him out.
He couldn't have performed.

My mother had only seen Hank that one time.
Christopher was pale
and Hank, deep black.
The only ones at the funeral were Doctor Clissold
and Oppy Pritchard, headmistress,
as well as the gravedigger who chucked on the soil.
Out of sight, out of mind.
I didn't go down to the church or churchyard,
not then, not thereafter.
I imagined the whereabouts of the grave.

Ernie wanted to know if he should tell Gus
to go over and get my mother.
"It's the right idea. She lives for Timmy
now that her own son is dead and gone."
So Ernie shouted to Gus to drive over.
Gus got into the ambulance.
The sound of the ambulance engine
was the sound of his objection
that once more he and Ernie were undergoing separation.

He wanted to be with Ernie.
Without me.
Without the hospital.
Without Timmy.
Without the *Dump*.
Without the war.

My mother's house was 6 miles outside Rhys,
so Gus had to drive 3 miles to our village, then another 3
to where Church Lane joined the main road.
Telephone pylon to electric pylon,
from the entrance to the rabbit's wood
to the next field gate,
each to each, in the pressed down headlights,

was a marked distance
wherein Gus was afraid that Ernie might find another,
and/or return to his pretty wife.

As we get older, never younger,
those miles of road from town to village
are a film rolling in the cinema of our heads.
By the time Gus drove me and my mother home,
the night was greyer.
The cloudscape with Hank and Hector billowing
was a place of violent whims.
Up there, pregnant, enlarged and grim
with a spider's agility
I was messing up the life inside me,
so Christopher would never whisper,
"Is this what breath is?"

Timmy came home two weeks later.
Two nurses brought him down to the bus station
in a wheel chair,
passed him a pair of crutches,
and put him on the bus.
He'd had no practice with those crutches,
he was certain he'd never get home,
that he'd never maneuver the getting-off.
With easy facility, the bus ate up the roadway,
then was swallowed by the hedges
that the roadsides heaved up.
Beyond the rear window there was a coming together,
then a dispreading.
The view receded as it was beginning.
And Timmy realized his life was too young
to be understood.

BOY

I'm transplanted
to and from a hospital that amounts to shapes
just about connected—
rotund fish in oblong pond,
square car belonging to long doctor parked in driveway,
sharp rectangular door in sharp hall, painted vain grey.
Uncle Hank (last face remembered before I came here)
would be able to arrange territories of village
territories of hospital
so that isolation would bloom into a bouquet.
But when I mention him, Mam's face goes crazy.
A forbidden finger to her lip conveys—Hank
cannot be revealed in any untoward expression,
words that come out must never include his name.

Now Phil Watkins is out in the village
neither to drink water from the village tap
nor to walk the streets.
He's out and about in the middle of the village
waiting for me to leave my dim morning origins,
to share the afternoon of this short vivid day.
I come along with a desire
to escape loneliness.
Loneliness is my scourge,
it muddies my waters,
darkens my days.
"Hello, Timmy. Do you want to play ball?"
"My leg's been hurt."
"I know. A stick went into it."
"But it's healed."
"Then let's play."

Phill holds a tough brown ball.
He lets the ball drop,
kicks the ball sideways to sideways, to delight me.

Expecting me to return it, he kicks it across.
There then, with its own life, it rolls down the hill
parallel to our garden wall. There,
where the garden wall finishes,
it rests in the gateway of an untended allotment.
Inside the gateway, exuberant weeds,
extravagant brussel sprouts.
I fetch the ball, run back up the hill, kick it over.
Phil returns it.
Again, it rushes by, decides to travel past the allotment,
rounding the turn at the bottom of the hill.
There then, then there,
it waits on the edge of ferns and nettles,
near the furry hollow tree
that's been growing for a few hundred years.
It shades Hector on his way home,
and Doctor Corner, trundling to and from his church.
It will shade any singular body,
tinged with the safety
of living 30 miles *north* of the capital city—
for during air raids 30 miles *south*,
bombs dive to suffocate the sky, to wound the earth.

Back up the hill once more,
if I kick the ball correctly
Phil Watkins might fall in love with me—
might want to marry me.
Thus is the afternoon of my beginnings,
the first afternoon of the first time
of Mam allowing me out alone.
"If you go out, the wound won't heal."
So I lie on my black iron bed in my back bedroom,
days packed with the mystery of new things
installed within the house since I've been away in hospital.
There's a new green carpet that snakes up the stairs.

Unlike the leftovers from Mrs. Colonel Probert,
this green snake covers the vertical
as well as the horizontal—
vertical to horizontal, horizontal to vertical,
is how steps understand themselves.
In Mam's front bedroom,
orange calico curtains flood the room with calico light.
Mam's white bedspread is an orange countryside.
Pillows are a calico mountain.
This calico mountain rises precisely, exactly, right.
Best, at the bottom of the stairs, a beaded curtain.
Coming at it, it is multi-colored tassels with tassels,
and it doesn't have to be cajoled into parting.
Automatically, throngs sweep forward along,
up from the kitchen, down from the stairs.

Food too, tins of vegetables, usually peas,
tins of meat, usually spam,
dried eggs and condensed milk,
all with colored labels.
Possibly this is war charity.
I know from the radio in the hospital
that recent battles have been won.
At night I hear a Voice,
the Voice and myself in the dark house will light up lights,
the Voice will hold me.
This Voice can be a Father.
A Father can be a Lover,
can be followed out of the valley
then up the mountains surrounding Rhys.
This Voice
will have to be searched for
up at the bus stop
down at the hut ground
inside the church.

When Mam allows me out,
the place I am to go to is the church.
"You are not to go up the road.
Go down to the church where I can see you.
Look around the graveyard.
Wait for me to come and get you.
Time will pass quickly if you behave yourself."
Inside the churchyard gate I should walk up the drive
through the lavender
into the graveyard proper
where ancient gravestones are fearfully conscious
of their subsidence into the soft earth.
The bull will look over the wall of its stall
to read inscriptions.
Try as he might, a bull can't decipher—
so he will make up a song:

> *I'll eat hay while the sun shines.*
> *If I make a noise after the sun sinks*
> *the owl from the yew tree*
> *will sweep down to peck out my eyes.*

Instead of playing ball with Phil
I should be down at the church.
But the village is pulsing
with the hope that I make Phil my friend.

As I come up the hill, I see another figure, Hector.
Hector is sitting on the wet stone
intended for water buckets.
He turns on the tap,
empties water over his head
that he's collected in his hand.
He is due to be chiseled.
He is a block of rock from the granite quarry,

sitting here just as he sits on his tractor,
waiting to be witnessed.
Alone with another
he'll use his mouth to kiss.
In company
his mouth only eats only breathes only speaks.

"Playing football, are you?"
Who is asking the question?
Is it Hector? It *is* Hector.
"Yeah."
Phil is kicking the ball, back and fro, back and fro,
against the side wall of our house.
I go across.
As I arrive at the spot where Phil could pass me the ball
and I could pass the ball back,
Hector comes from behind, picks me up,
his arms around the middle of me,
forcing breath down to my stomach, up to my throat.
Underneath the soles of my feet,
Hector kicks the ball back to Phil.
Puts me down.
Goes back to his rock.
"Can't get at the ball, can you, fella!"
"Course I can't get to the ball if you pick me up!"
I go back towards Phil
hoping an afternoon spirit will instruct Hector to follow.
He does follow. He does pick me up. Again.
The simplicity of the act is designed to be repeated—
except, when the ball rolls down the hill,
he follows after.
Well, hell!
Can't tell if he's following the ball or pell-mell walking off.

He's gonna go, past allotment, past hut ground,

past hollow tree, past church—
gonna lock himself in his farm house
because life outside
is too heavy with choices.
Momentarily I settle on a large decision.
I'll alter Hector's reasoning,
mold his torments,
re-fashion his concerns.

Purposefully, the ball rolls beyond Hector
to lodge in the entrance of the allotment.
Gates are five-bar-wood, five-bar-iron.
Iron of iron gates to private houses
is fashioned into crosses,
but not *this* twig-wooden fabrication,
noticeably intricate, noticeably weak—
not to be passionate against,
nor to be lovingly leant on.

Therefore
we are forced to stand front to each other's front
without support,
listening—
our blood cells whispering,
"Enjoy this chaos.
It is indigenous.
It is to be endured."

Looking at Hector
there is the top of his dark hair with no parting,
the wonder of his being older yet shorter,
me younger yet taller,
his hands on my waist,
my two hands around his shoulders,
touching the broadness.

His muscles getting stronger.
Me, discombobulating,
yet becoming what I am.

"Eh, Fella! Better tell Phill you don't want go on playing."
His words forge chains around my chest, my groin.
"Your ball's in the gateway of the allotment," I shout.
"Come and get it."
Phil recedes into the past
even as he advances to get his ball.

I pull Hector to the bottom of the hill,
drag him around the corner,
away from one window in one small house
that overlooks—
a square-foot pane, under the eaves,
all eye all glass all light all ray
in the afternoon no wave of sound.

I drag Hector through the gap beside the furry hollow tree
into the hut ground.
Like the summer grasses, we are full of seed yet powdery.
Since the outbreak of war
we have not been pruned.

Down in the delightful grass,
plants are smothered.
Sunflowers and blue foxgloves stretch up
to embrace a sequel to their blossoming,
a prequel to their getting old.

Hector walks ahead
to where the ground of the hut ground,
the hut ground's ground, slants.
A brook a river a sun a pond a group of moor hens

a railway bridge a railway line
watch Hector take off his trousers then his underpants.
On the slanting bank, the raw length of him
is instantly supportive to his cock.

This man thing of him, not designed for self-sufficiency,
is happy with my company.
"Ready, Fella?
I'm gonna put this inside you.
It'll fill you up.
When I get this inside you,
I will be the man really meant for you."

I am a scruffy soldier,
Hector is a warrior,
the available Hero on this bank.

"Can you feel me?"
"Yeah."
(Though nowhere inside.)
His man thing thrusts
in a fond lodged situation that is located between my legs,
not up my ass.

Nevertheless, he's wonderfully lunging.
"How far inside?"
"In my stomach."
"In your stomach! Jesus Christ!"
Both of us are insanely excited by my lies.

He turns me over. I'm spidery. My legs are in the air.
"Now do you feel a difference?"
The sky leers and peers,
the soft ground heaves.
I say I feel a difference.
In truth, there *is* a tunneling in my fundament.

But I'm unsure if Hector is tunneling
into my stomach or into my mind.

Ecstasy knocks out my eyes.
Covers up my earholes.
Intermittently and painfully
I am blissfully deaf and blind.

On the slant
on a wild bank
I belong to the peasantry—
a heap of a peasant lying on the slant
on a bank in slanting Wales.

When I maneuver down under his lovely body,
it is my mouth that is looking,
my mouth searching Hector's hairy lollopy slollops,
his slollopy hairy lollops
related to the allotment's knobbly sprouts.
"I suppose you want to kiss them?
I suppose you want to lick them?"
I lick them with the tongue
that lives in the cavity of my largest mouth.
A nearby dandelion
ascertains degrees of pleasure.
"Pretended pleasure is the same only different."
That's what the dandelion believes it's found out.

Above, in the shape of a crow
a farmer's son
watches a young Welsh fella
capturing the taste
of the farmer's son's
mound of testicle
insistent dick

urgent cum.

In the turbulence after
the excretion of Hector's great event,
Hector puts on his clothes.
Before reaching outside the hut-ground
he disappears down a fox-hole—
there are maybe a dozen fox-holes in the hut-ground,
holes in the earth for the home guard
to burrow into further darkness
in the chock-dark night.
Lonely young men
who've shown off their dicks
are encouraged into the daylight fox-hole
to explain their activities out a gun turret window.
Hector makes a promise—
"All parts of my body
singly and tingly
will visit all the village
in the ongoing course of my inner life."

As for me, as I travel back to the village street.
I remember Hector telling me,
"You swallowed, you tasted me.
You're going to get into terrible trouble."
"What'll they do to me?"
"They'll send you to prison."
Now my house, at the top of the hill
bestows a judgment:
"Hector, the only young man in the village,
is the victim of an overall boredom.
And *you* have taken advantage.
You are to blame."

The curtains across Mam's bedroom window

are severely drawn—
protecting the inside
from this outside,
protecting that room
from this afternoon.
Our small house stands sturdily.
Our landlord is a pig farmer
with a daughter as strong as a strongman.

Back in the day
she bought a packet of seeds.
One of the seeds, individual as the day I was born,
grew into the exact house
pictured on the packet.
The germ of the seed
decided Mam's skin under her dress
should be orange-rind white,
while Uncle Hank under his uniform
would remain the brightest ebony.
The packet also stipulated
Mam and Uncle Hank should lie sideways facing,
and their lengths should be similar
to my length as I lay under Hector.
The packet of the exact house
stipulated that this was a condition
known as *bliss.*

I open the back door and hear an upstairs murmuring.
Thinking this is Mam talking to herself,
I open her bedroom door to say,
"I'm back.
Don't worry. I've kept myself to myself."

Mam lies on the bed sideways towards Uncle Hank.
She's in a flowered dress

and reminds me of a mother
lying sideways in the midst of flowers
on the bank of a river.
Uncle Hank, in his uniform and tie,
is the naked black man
who lights lamps.
Also, he is Hector
who disorders order.
I've made him sharp cos I am blunt.

"Uncle Hank came by to see if your leg is better."
"Is your leg better, Fella?"
"Yeah. Thanks."
"The thing is . . . Uncle Hank . . .
has had . . . a nasty accident himself.
Let me show you."

Uncle Hank allows her
to take his over-sized hand, bring it across.
The interior of Uncle Hank's hand has the creaminess
of a pool of thick milk.
In the center of the pool is a large black spot.
"A thorn has gone into his hand.
I don't want you to see me getting it out."
"That's not a thorn. That's a birthmark.
I've got one on my leg."
"It's a thorn! And I don't want you watching!"
"Why not?"
"It will hurt him. You'll be frightened by that."
"I will not."
"I might cry and shout," warns Uncle Hank.
"It's best for you not to see. It's best for you to go out."
"Where? I'm fed up with the church."
"Go to the pub."
"I'm too small."

"With this, you're not."
He puts his hand into his trouser pocket
and brings out a bright half-crown.
"What shall I drink?"
"A shandy."
"What's that?"
"Lemonade with cider, or lemonade with stout."

I walk up the street
in the direction my black uncle has directed.
Stones in the walls
press out against their mortar boundaries
as I sit on the five-bar wooden gate opposite the school—
church, hut-ground, Hector's farm,
Doctor Corner in his rectory,
furry hollow tree, allotment, brussel sprouts,
all travel past
fast as American jeeps,
as German bombs.
Hank will be with Mam on the calico bed
when the village, on the way to obliteration,
is smashed to smithereens.

I jump off the gate into the field,
descend into a brook.
Banks on all sides rise steeply from the water.
Above, in the fields, the gash of the brook
is hidden by briared bushes
growing in a profused state.
From the sky, the brook is hidden
by the top foliage of trees
growing into their roots high down in the earth.
In the brook, out of the dry-keeping of my being,
I go from stone to stone—
for a time remaining on top the water,

though down here
there's a stone then another stone
with no continuing step between.
Under such conditions I fall,
commune with tadpoles bigger than the frogs
who claim to be their parents.
I'm smitten by the strong will of my own wishes.
I'm kissed by eels slimier than snakes.

From the brook I clamber back up to the field
with a quish-quash walk,
exiting to the squelching road.
On the right the pub is waiting.
Military jeeps parked outside exist in too much detail.
They think today's the day, tonight's gonna be the night.
Corners of the pub edge out,
expecting battle.
It's all show.
This *King of Prussia* pub is a thing.
Things can't fight.

Inside, voices come from other rooms.
Angles have disappeared.
Webs with threads come to the fore.
Behind the bar, Branwen, the daughter-in-law,
stands among the casks of heavy beer.

"What do you want?"
She is beery with thinning hair.
"I want a shandy. Half cider, half lemonade."
"What a state you're in! Look at your clothes!"
Her voice is strong with the wish not to be ignored.
She takes me back to the back kitchen
where old Ma West, her mother-in-law,
sits silhouetted by the light from the garden

beyond the open door.
"Ma. Here's Timmy. You know Timmy!"
"Why's he here?"
Ma's white hair, along with her blossoming soft body,
lives in this dark kitchen.
Whereas the sun itself can't get in the door.
That's for sure. The sun is sure.

I am a straight-stander permitted to stand in front of her.
(Her daughter-in-law is a straight-stander
who belongs to the bar.)
"I've come for a shandy, half lemonade, half cider."
I pull out my half-crown.
"Goodness! Where did you get that?"
"My Mam."
"Mam gave you half a crown?"
"Mam didn't. It was my Black Uncle. He's a soldier.
Mam is getting a thorn out of his hand at the moment.
They think I might be frightened,
so they told me to come here."
"Get him a shandy," she tells her daughter-in-law.
"Where are they?"
"Who?"
"Mammy and this black soldier."
"Sitting on the bed, at home."
"Look at the state you are in. Let me dry you!
—Desmond!" she calls, "Bring me a towel!
And a pair of your old trousers!
And a shirt!"
Desmond is her old-man son—
whenever he passes us waiting for the bus
he pokes his head out his car window to yell,
"What you all looking at?"
And, looking at the nothing beyond nothing beyond
nothing, he drives on.

Desmond brings in the towel and clothes.
Branwen brings in my shandy.
Then Ma West tells them to get out.
"I'm going to take off his clothes."

Ma West stands me naked between her knees.
Is it her or the big towel that engulfs me?
I am enveloped in the mystery.
She is the oldest being I've ever been this close up to.
Does she want to feel me
because I am almost-not-quite a man?
"Who is this black man?"
"He's my Black Uncle."
"You can't have a black uncle."
"I can show you."
"Why are you so wet?"
"I came up by the brook."
"God in heaven! You came up by the brook
because you're upset."

"Desmond!
Take the car over to Chapel Lane, to Tim's Gran.
Her house is in the orchard, opposite the chapel.
Bring her back with you.
We've got to let her know what's going on."
She holds my head within the towel
and makes it dance between her mighty tits.
"Let me dry you.
Too much dampness will destroy you."
I'm waiting for the unpredictable
but she only says,
"Put these clothes on
and walk around the garden."
Guilt for having yapped my yap to her
spreads all round the garden,

goes down to a great depth.
The realization of betraying secrets
attaches heavily.
Bean stalks remain on their skeletal frames
long after the gathering of the crop.

Old Ma West joins Branwen in the bar
when Desmond returns with Gran.
Gran and Ma West come into the kitchen.
Gran waves her wave that says:
"You are on no account to age,
you are to remain compliantly the same
no matter what is going on."
After a quick chat with Ma West, Gran leaves quickly—
through the garden hedge I see her
going towards the village,
through the field she is striding.
Towards an assignation?
She's gonna bend bent branches straight,
gonna turn troublesome night into untroubled day.

In the bar, Branwen, Ma West, Desmond,
mingle with American soldiers.
"I'm going home," I yell in a radio voice
that declares
beginnings and conclusions
only appertaining to me.

I rush back to the field.
Gran, at the other end, is poised,
in the act of wondering—
"Why, instead of going through the gate,
am I climbing o'er the stile?"
Also—
"Never have I met a black man!

Never touched a black child."

To follow her I run down along the path
alongside the brook.
I came up by this brook,
this brook encased by briared bushes
and low enveloping trees.
With curved shadows bending, depth is a detour.
But this path, the color of hard mud,
running between the brook
and the cultivated edge of the planted field
is not a detour.
And though there are no straight lines in nature,
it's gonna take me direct to the wooden fence and stile
opposite the school on the village street.

I sit on the stile.
The field behind me (the field I've walked through)
has recently been harvested.
Men excused from the war
along with land-girls
come to help, stacking the sheaves of wheat
after the combine harvester spews them out.
The towering machine, rented along with its gristled driver,
eats the perimeter,
reducing the gold expanse of the field inexorably
into smaller, then smaller plots.
When the plot is absurdly central, tidily tiny,
out come the rabbits.
They have only a few breaths left to spare.
Splitting apart from compressed nature
they dash singly in multitudes towards
brook pub sky school river.
Old Man Rodgers Hector Steer Farmer Pig Killer
have all taken out their guns.

They don't get all of them, just many of them,
changing the elasticity of the rabbits
as they stretch towards survival
into the electrical unconscious
of dead imploding dots.

Hank, my Black Uncle, strides.
Gran has bundled him out of the house onto the street.
He no longer lingers
in the darkness of hedges,
there's no more maneuvering along hidden precipitations.
Gran has shoved him out,
into a disputed freedom
where the sun highlights muscles
developed from the bruising inflicted on his ancestors
for more than four hundred years.
Villagers, staring from behind net curtains,
stroke their privates
(Welsh villagers can possess as many
as fifty-five to sixty private parts)
excited that this black soldier might be out to attack.

Revenge might come later.
Now he is exhausted from having fertilized my mother.
The village heard Hank's sperm
swimming up the fallopian tube towards Mam's egg.
Then animals,
in this case swans,
on any pond,
way inland,
ponder.
The shape in Mam's uterus amounts to a fetus
the size of a grain of rice.
In terms of the evolution of a Welsh black race,
this is early on.

For when it comes out from Mam's belly,
the babe (named Christopher, after Christ)
is granted only four days of life.
Breath comes in snatches.
Features are black.
Skin is white.
For those four anxious days he is too small.

A short life is appreciated
when the babe lies in its coffin.
Gran brings me into the front bedroom.
The baby's closed eyes look at the ceiling,
Mam lies in her bed with her face to the wall.
Gran says, "Now you've seen him,
you're never to ask *where is Christopher gone?*"
I don't know how the tiny coffin gets to the graveyard,
nor who makes the decision for the grave to be dug
where the sweeping outward branches of the yew
touch the ground.
The mound of the grave is bare bones adequate,
too small to commemorate.
In a matter of two pure short months,
the grave is gone.

Years later, I'm studying in the capital.
Some weekends I come home.
Post-war train travels past
transient realities.
Houses are mole hills in fields
which can't be grasped—
for the village chucks up against the window
(distance means nothing in this sleek train)
the jigsaw of my young life,
chucks it across the pane.
Conglomeration of water is the river.

Conglomeration of stone and brick is the village.
The jigsaw is further put together
by a grandmother climbing a stile,
a youth and a boy fascinated one to another,
a yew tree, compounded of the remains of corpses,
a bull watching the grave of a four-day old baby
over the wall of its stall.

I'm hoping he's going to look at me,
but Hank passes as if there's not enough space.
"I'm not dangerous. I'm not Hitler."
"In daylight I am whiter, you are blacker."
"Was it you who bought the beaded curtain?"
"Do you still want to go for a drive in the mountains?"
Hank passes without speaking.
I'll have to share myself with myself.
"Do you want to meet my friend? His name is Hector."
"Are you leaving forever?"

A black soldier, fighting a white man's war,
waits up at a bus-stop.
A white student, studying white literature
in the white capitol,
searches out a train window.

What's next?

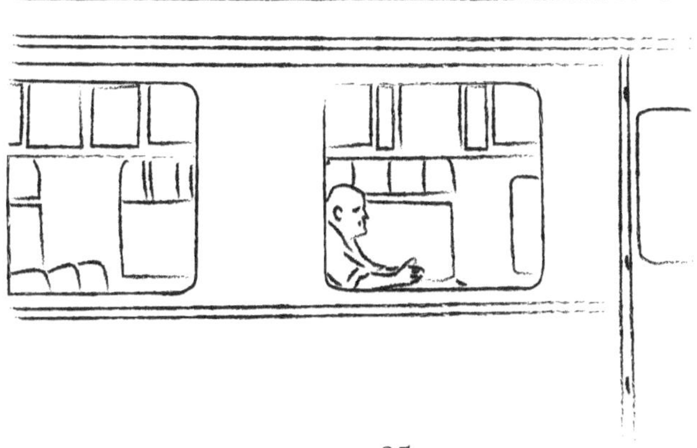

About The Author

Born in Wales, John Marcus Powell has lived in London, Paris, Rome, Algeria, and for the past quarter of a century in New York City. His career as an actor spans British Rep, British soaps (Emergency Ward 10), London's West-End (Zigger-Zagger), Off-Broadway (The Comedians, Perfect Crime) Off-Off-Broadway (Hedda Gabler, The Visit), and American Horror movies (Metamorphosis: The Alien Factor). In London, he was directed by Harold Pinter in Robert Shaw's The Man In The Glass Booth. He is the author of a chapbook, Loonie Lovers, (EXOT BOOKS, 2012), and two full length poetry collections, also from EXOT BOOKS, Glorious Babe (2014) and Veil On, Veil Off (2018). He continues to perform his poetry in New York City with a flair that is unmistakably his own. As a poet he tap-dances to the rhythms of verse & prose, boogies through transgression, jives with socialism, square-dances with queerness, and flirts with any anarchic poet he's ever encountered. He plans to live almost forever.

Other Titles Available From Exot Books

Pools of June, Mary Meriam ~ 2022
Huncke, Rick Mullin ~ 2021
Schnauzer, David Yezzi ~ 2018
Veil On, Veil Off, John Marcus Powell ~ 2018
A Special Education, Meredith Bergmann ~ 2014
Glorious Babe, John Marcus Powell ~ 2014
Questions, Richard Loranger/Bill Mercer ~ 2013
Turn, Ann Drysdale ~ 2013
Tomorrow & Tomorrow, David Yezzi ~ 2013
Facing The Remains, Tom Merrill ~ 2012
Blue Wins Forever, Paco Brown ~ 2012
They Can Keep The Cinderblock, Mike Lane ~ 2012
Colors, Jay Chollick ~ 2011
Loony Lovers, John Marcus Powell ~ 2011
Filled With Breath: 30 Sonnets by 30 Poets, ed. Mary Meriam ~ 2010
Let Me Be Like Glass, Adriana Scopino ~ 2010
What's That Supposed To Mean, Wendy Videlock ~ 2010
We Internet In Different Voices, Mike Alexander ~ 2009
11 Films, Jane Ormerod ~ 2008
Aquinas Flinched, Rick Mullin ~ 2008
Graceways, Austin MacRae ~ 2008
Prospero At Breakfast, Alan Wickes ~ 2008
Sometime Before The Bell, Ray Pospisil ~ 2006
The Countess Of Flatbroke, Mary Meriam ~ 2006
Blue Glass Cities, Mark Allinson ~ 2006
Prolegomena To An Essay On Satire, R. Nemo Hill ~2006
William Montgomery, Quincy R. Lehr ~ 2006

ORDER ONLINE AT exotbooks.com

www.ingramcontent.com/pod-product-compliance
Lightning Source LLC
Chambersburg PA
CBHW021705110726
47902CB00007B/2067